Word List

Here is a list of words that might make it easier
to read this book. You'll find them in boldface
the first time they appear in the story.

tongues	tungz
superstitious	soo-per-STI-shuhs
alternate	AWL-ter-nit
dormitory	DOR-muh-tor-ee
Sorbonne	sor-BOHN
Eiffel	EYE-fuhl
holograms	HOL-uh-gramz
chrysanthemums	kri-SAN-thuh-mumz
jealous	JE-luhs
Palais de Neige	pal-AY duh nejj
Australian	aw-STRAYL-yuhn
concentration	kon-suhn-TRAY-shun

Barbie™

Danizhu(

The Lucky Skates

BARBIE and associated trademarks are owned by and used under license from Mattel, Inc. © 1998 Mattel, Inc. All Rights Reserved. Published by Grolier Books, a division of Grolier Enterprises, Inc. Story by Jacqueline A. Ball and Patsy Jensen. Photo crew: Jeff O'Brien, Vince Okada, Mary Hirahara, Patrick Kittel, and Lisa Collins. Produced by Bumpy Slide Books. Printed in the United States of America.

ISBN: 0-7172-8827-7

GROLIER
B O O K S

Chapter One

Coach Barbie stood at the edge of the skating rink watching Allie Moreno. Allie spun and leapt on the ice. She looked like a dancing moonbeam in her silver tights.

Allie was a good skater. Actually, Allie was an outstanding skater. She had won almost every major figure skating event all year. But now came the real test. How would she do here in Paris, France, at the World SuperSkate Championship?

Suddenly Allie began to pick up speed.

Barbie held her breath. She knew what was coming: Allie's trademark combination jump. It

was the one reporters had nicknamed the
"Allie-Oop."

"Ready for liftoff," Barbie said to herself.

Allie's skates slashed across the ice. Then
she was high in the air, twisting and turning like a
tornado. One turn . . . two turns . . . three turns!
A perfect triple axel!

Allie landed perfectly. She glided backward
for a moment. Then she immediately began
picking up speed again.

"One down, one to go," whispered Barbie.

Faster . . . faster . . . and then three more
thrilling midair spins.

A perfect triple toe loop!

"ALLIE-OOP!" Barbie cheered.

Allie's move was one of the most difficult
combinations a figure skater could do. It was
also very risky. That's why audiences loved it,
and why judges gave Allie the highest scores
in competitions. Those scores had combined to

rank her as the number one skater in the world.

Allie skated over to the rail. "Did you see me nail those triples, Coach?" she asked Barbie. Allie was out of breath, but smiling.

"You were excellent!" exclaimed Barbie. "Your form and timing have never been better. All that hard work is really paying off!"

Assistant Coach Christie joined them. "Too bad this is only a practice," she said. "But in a couple of days, it will be the real thing. The short programs are scheduled for Sunday."

Figure skaters competed in two different programs. For the short program, they all performed the same eight moves in two minutes and forty seconds. The long program was called freestyle. Skaters chose whichever jumps and turns they wanted and created a four-minute routine. Both programs had music and beautiful costumes.

Allie grinned. "With Barbie for a coach and these lucky skates, how can I go wrong?" she said.

Allie patted the **tongues** of her skates.

Everyone knew how **superstitious** Allie was about this particular pair of skates. Since she had started wearing them, she had been unbeatable.

Barbie smiled and put her hand on Allie's shoulder. "It's talent, skill, and hard work that got you here, not good luck charms. Believe in yourself, not your skates."

Allie shrugged. "Here comes Julia," she said, trying to change the subject.

"She looks tired," said Barbie. "The time difference between here and home takes getting used to. After all, it's six hours later here in Paris."

A girl with copper-colored curls skated up to them. She was frowning and rubbing her arm.

"I don't know what's wrong with me," Julia said. "I'm falling down more than ever before. Could the ice be super-rough or something?"

Two years ago, Julia Kelly had been the top figure skater in the world. But when Allie joined the team, Julia's scores had started to sink. She had barely made the SuperSkate team.

Just then a tiny skater coasted to the rail. "It's the same ice Allie was on, Julia," she teased. Her eyes sparkled with fun. "And *she* wasn't falling."

"Now, Pam," Barbie said, "don't tease. We're a team, remember? We all have to stick together."

"I'm only kidding," Pam said. Pam Chen was the youngest member of the team. At fifteen, she was one of the youngest athletes in the entire competition. And at four-foot-ten, she was also one of the shortest. "Sorry, Barbie. Sorry, Julia," she said.

Julia sighed. "Oh, don't worry about it, Pam. Let's face it. I'm having a bad practice." She made a face. "Maybe I should borrow Allie's lucky skates!"

Just then, Meg Carlson joined them.

"If anyone needs lucky skates, it's me," she said as she leaned against the rail, chin on her hands. "I'm only an **alternate.** I'll need some kind of luck to skate at all."

Pam laughed. "Wait a second!" she said. "We love you, Meg, but the only way you can skate is if one of us drops out. That would be *bad* luck for us!"

"Well, it doesn't matter. Nobody is going to use these skates but me," said Allie.

Barbie folded her arms. "Listen, guys, there is no such thing as a lucky pair of skates. Allie has worked very, very hard over the past year. *That's* why she's skating so well. It doesn't matter which skates are on her feet."

Allie looked down at the ice.

"Julia, you probably just need more rest," Barbie continued. "Try to focus on how hard you've been training lately. I think you've got the stuff to knock 'em dead here. And Meg, please don't think of yourself as 'only an alternate.' You're *much* more than that! You're part of a terrific, talented team. If you don't get to compete this time, your turn will come. Trust me."

The skaters were quiet. Barbie always made so much sense.

"Everyone feel better?" Barbie asked, smiling. The girls nodded.

"Anyone for lunch?" Christie asked.

"You're on!" exclaimed Pam.

"Let's go!" said Julia.

"I'm starving!" declared Meg.

"I'll join you in a few minutes," said Allie. "I just have to wipe off my skates and put them away."

The cafeteria at International House was on the college campus where the competition was being held. It was always a busy place. Open day and night, the cafeteria served a huge variety of foods. Students and athletes could choose from many kinds of meals. There were foods from all of the countries and cultures taking part in the competition. There was also plenty of French food for the students who lived in the dorms.

"Pizza!" exclaimed Allie. "This is my lucky day!"

The girls filled their trays with pizzas, small sandwiches, and yogurts. They had been working hard all morning and were very hungry. After lunch they walked over to the women's **dormitory.**

The men's and women's dormitories, or *dorms,* were like hotels. In addition to the students' rooms, there were enough single and double rooms to hold hundreds of athletes. Julia and Allie walked to the room they shared, across the hall from Pam and Meg's room. Barbie and Christie each had her own room down the hall. Everyone piled into Julia and Allie's room.

"I've got an idea," said Barbie. "Let's take a break from practice and do some shopping and sightseeing."

"Great idea!" exclaimed Pam. "I've been dying to get some new stickers."

Pam collected stickers. She had hundreds, in every color, shape, and size.

"I told my grandma I would bring her back a birthday present from Paris," said Julia.

"And I told my brother I would get him something," added Allie. "His birthday's next week. I need a present for Mom and Dad, too. And, of course, I can't forget Hammie."

"I didn't know you had a hamster," Meg said.

"I don't," Allie answered. "Hammie is my cat. I named her after Dorothy Hamill. You know, the champion skater—"

"From the '70s," Julia finished.

"But did she win championships with or without lucky skates?" Pam asked with a laugh.

Allie tossed a pillow at her teammate. "Cut it out, Pam!"

Barbie sighed. "Enough! Not one more word about lucky skates!"

"Okay. Let's talk about shoes instead," Meg

suggested. "Everyone looks so great here in Paris, I need a new look. Hey, Julia, may I wear your pink loafers to go shopping?"

"Sure," Julia replied, "if Allie will loan *me* her blue ones."

"Okay," said Allie, "if you'll loan *me* your clogs, Meg."

"I guess I'll wear my old high-tops," said Pam with a sigh. "You guys are so lucky you're the same size."

"It's not our fault you have such small feet!" Meg told her.

The girls giggled. Then Barbie, Christie, and the team headed out to see the sights of Paris.

Chapter Two

The campus where the athletes were staying was part of a big university called the **Sorbonne.** It was located just outside the center of Paris. To get to the city, the athletes would take the subway, or *metro,* as it was called in France.

After a short ride, the team got off and climbed up the stairs into the daylight. It was a clear day, and in the distance they could see the **Eiffel** Tower glimmering in the sunlight. The wide, tree-lined streets were crowded with fashionable, busy people.

Each small shop sold something special. One

had all different kinds of bread. Another had sweet pastries and cookies. Another had nothing but fancy chocolates piled high on silver trays.

Allie immediately stopped outside the chocolate shop. "Hey, guys," she began, "what do you think about some French chocolates for my little brother?"

"Sounds good. But let's go look inside that cool bread shop first," said Meg, pointing across the street.

Barbie laughed. "Why don't we split up to shop and meet back here later?"

"Good idea!" said Allie and Meg together.

Barbie took one group, and Christie took the other. They all met up later at a little sidewalk café

Julia showed everyone a red and yellow silk scarf she had bought. "I know Gran will love it," she said.

Pam had bought long strips of stickers. Some were **holograms** that flashed and shifted shapes when she moved them. Others glittered with gold

14

and silver. "These flower stickers are my favorites," she said.

Everyone looked at the stickers she held.

"They look like **chrysanthemums,**" said Allie.

"Or like snowballs," Meg said. "Can I have a couple, Pam?"

"Sure," Pam answered. She tore off a strip with two stickers and handed it to Meg.

Barbie looked closely at the pretty design. "They remind me of our team," she said. "It takes a lot of petals to make one beautiful flower!"

"Well, they sure are pretty," added Meg. She brushed some stray blond hairs out of her eyes and stuck her strip of stickers in the pocket of her jacket.

Back at the campus, the team hopped off the metro. Suddenly a crowd of reporters and fans gathered around them.

"Allie-Oop!" someone called from the crowd.

"Hey, Allie! Over here!"

"Allie, Allie!" yelled another voice. "Sign this picture!"

A TV reporter pushed a microphone in front of Allie's face. "How about it, Allie? Feeling lucky enough to bring home first place?"

Allie cleared her throat. She was used to being interviewed. Reporters had been following her all year.

"Well, my coach, Barbie, has really helped me this year," Allie began, "so I'm feeling great. And of course, I have my lucky skates! I couldn't win without them."

Allie signed autographs while the others waited. Finally a reporter turned to Julia. "How are you feeling, Julia?"

"I'm feeling as if I could use some lucky skates, too!" Julia said with a short laugh. "If only to get a little attention around here!" she said softly

Barbie was concerned. Despite her laughter,

Julia sounded **jealous.**

Barbie made her way through the crowd. "Enough questions," she told the reporters firmly. "These girls need their rest and practice time." She stood behind the team and put her hands on their shoulders. "But let me say that everyone on this team is a champion. Allie, Julia, Pam, and Meg make up the best American women's SuperSkate team ever."

"But only one can win the first-place trophy," a reporter called out.

"Yeah, only one can be lucky enough," Julia said to herself as they left.

Chapter Three

"Can you believe how many people were out there?" exclaimed Meg, flopping down on her bed.

Barbie was with the team in Pam and Meg's room. Julia sat at the desk. She played with her coppery ponytail as she stared into space. Allie lay on the floor doing leg lifts. Pam was carefully placing stickers into a large album.

Barbie cleared her throat. "Look, guys, let's clear the air. Allie's gotten all the attention lately, and I know that's tough for the rest of you. But it's not her fault. Besides, we're a team. We have to be there for each other, on and off the ice. Let's focus

18

on the practice sessions and not let anything else get in the way." Barbie looked straight at Julia. "Is that a deal, Julia?" she asked.

Julia nodded slowly. "Sure," she said.

The others nodded, too.

"Good!" said Barbie. "Now Christie and I are going over to the recording studio. We need to approve all your music." Then Barbie stood up and put on her jacket. "Allie, don't forget, we have that TV interview in an hour."

Allie jumped up. "Oh, gosh! I *did* forget! I'd better get ready. Meet you there, Barbie." She raced out the door and across the hall to her room.

"Oh, and I almost forgot," Christie said to the others. "You need to get your skates sharpened this afternoon. Leave them in one place in the locker room. I'll pick them up and bring them over to the sharpening shop while Allie and Barbie do the interview. Use your backup pair of skates for practice. Julia, would you mind bringing Allie's?"

"No problem," replied Julia. "No problem at all."

A few hours later, Barbie entered the *Palais de Neige,* the huge championship skating center near the campus. This was where the competitions would be held. She found Christie there watching the skaters.

"How's it going, Christie? Any problems?" Barbie asked.

"Everything's fine," replied Christie. "The skates are at the sharpening shop. Someone from the shop will bring them back here. Pam's having a great session. Julia is looking fabulous. She seems to have come out of her slump."

Barbie noticed Meg doing slow, graceful spirals with one leg stretched behind her. "Meg looks good, too," she said.

"Yes," replied Christie. "Finally."

"What do you mean, 'finally'?" asked Barbie

"She was having a bad day," Christie

explained. "She was skating poorly. Then her ponytail holder broke. When she returned to the ice, she fell four times in about five minutes. I left to bring the team's skates to the sharpener's. When I came back, Meg was doing much better. And you're right. She looks excellent now."

"I wonder what caused the change," Barbie said. She glanced around the rink. "I also wonder why Allie isn't out there. She went to her room after the interview, but that was a long time ago."

"Here she comes now," said Christie. "Uh-oh. She looks upset."

"My lucky skates are missing!" Allie cried. "Someone took my lucky skates!"

"Hold on, Allie," said Barbie. "Calm down."

Allie looked nervous. "How can I be calm when my lucky skates are gone?"

"Take it easy," said Christie gently. "Your skates are at the sharpener's. I brought them there myself from the locker room."

Allie looked puzzled. "But how did they get to the locker room? I didn't bring them."

"Julia did. I asked her to," said Christie.

"Well, she could have told me she was taking them!" Allie burst out.

"I did. But you were in the shower," said Julia, skating up to join them. "You must not have heard me. Too busy getting ready for your one-millionth interview."

"Please, Julia. You're not helping," Barbie told her.

"Well, we're all getting sick of hearing about her 'lucky' skates," Julia said angrily. "Can you blame us?" She skated away.

Just then a young man set down four gym bags in front of the bench. "All set, Coach," he told Barbie. "Nice and sharp, for that special champion edge."

"Hurray!" exclaimed Allie. Eagerly she grabbed her gold gym bag and pulled out a pair of skates. Allie laced up the skates, removed the plastic guards, and soon she was dancing across the ice. A happy smile lit up her face.

But a few minutes later she fell hard, right on her backside.

"Ouch!" Allie shouted.

"Are you okay?" Barbie called.

"I think so," Allie said. She got up and skated slowly to the rail. "But my skates feel funny. I'd better relace them."

She sat down on a bench and took off the skates. Suddenly she cried, "Hey! These aren't my lucky skates!"

Barbie came over to her. "What? Are you sure?"

"Yes," Allie said. She pointed under the tongue of one skate. "There's no heart here. My mom and dad drew a heart on the inside of each of my lucky skates. That way I'll know they're thinking about me wherever I go."

Allie was shaking now as tears streamed

down her face. "My lucky skates really *are* missing! Someone stole them!"

"Maybe the hearts just wore off," Barbie suggested.

"No," said Allie firmly. "I *know* the hearts still show. I check them every day. They're like a hug from my parents."

Suddenly Allie stopped crying. "Wait a minute! I know what might have happened!" Allie glared out at Julia, who was skating perfectly. Allie was furious. "Julia could have switched my skates with hers. She's trying to steal my skates *and* my luck! And my trophy!"

"Allie!" gasped Barbie. "I'm shocked that you would accuse a teammate of something like that! This must be just a mix-up."

"We'll check everything out after practice, in the locker room," promised Christie.

"But Barbie, what am I going to do?" Allie cried. "I can't compete without my lucky skates!"

Barbie spoke calmly. "We'll do everything we can to help you find your skates, Allie. But right now, it's important that you understand you're a champion, with or without that pair of skates."

Allie looked very unhappy. "I don't feel like a champion without my lucky skates," she said.

Barbie lifted Allie's chin and looked right into her eyes. "You *are* a champion, and it's because you're talented and a very hard worker! It's not because of your skates! Now, why don't you take a break? We'll get to the bottom of this."

Allie slumped down on the bench. In the rink, Julia completed a perfect triple axel. She almost floated back down to the ice.

"Looking good, Julia!" someone called. "What's your secret?"

"Maybe my luck is finally changing," she called back. Then she skated around the rink with both thumbs up and a big smile across her face.

Chapter Four

When the practice session was over, Barbie
called for a team meeting in the locker room.

"Allie's skates are missing," Barbie explained
to the team. "The ones that came back from the
sharpener's are her backups. As you know, the
missing skates have hearts drawn inside the tongue
Everyone, please look to see that you have your
own skates. They may have gotten mixed up at
the sharpener's. Meg, please check that top row
of lockers. Pam, help me check these."

The group searched the locker room. They
looked under benches and even in the shower

room. But Allie's skates did not turn up.

"Did you look in every locker?" asked Barbie.

"All except the ones that were locked," Meg said.

"Wait a minute. This one isn't locked," said Christie. "It's just stuck." She yanked open a locker in the top row.

"It's empty!" declared Meg.

Then something fluttered down to the floor. Christie leaned down and picked up a sticker with a white chrysanthemum on it.

"Isn't this your sticker, Pam?" she asked.

"It looks like one that I bought," Pam said. She scratched her head. "But mine are all back in the dorm, in my album."

"Another mystery," Barbie pointed out. "Let's retrace our steps. Julia, was anyone else here when you dropped off the skates?"

"Not then. But when I came back later, I saw the **Australian** coach here," replied Julia.

"Well, I'll talk to her," said Barbie. "Maybe one of her team members noticed something."

Suddenly Julia pulled her jacket out of the locker and threw it across her shoulders. She yawned. "You know, I'm really beat, Barbie. I'd like to take a nap before dinner. May I go now?"

"I'm tired, too," Pam chimed in. "And I wanted to call home."

"Of course," said Barbie. "See you later."

Only Meg stayed behind. "Your skates will turn up, Allie," she said. She put her arm around her teammate. "I'm sure of it."

But Allie was still very upset.

"I'm sure, too," Barbie told her. "I'm just not sure when. We'll keep looking for them, but I want you to start using your backup skates."

"I guess I have no choice," said Allie sadly.

That night, Barbie knocked on Julia and Allie's door. When Allie opened it, Barbie could tell she had been crying.

"I'm sorry, Allie," Barbie said gently. "The missing skates weren't at the sharpener's."

Allie tried to hold back her tears. "I keep trying not to think about it, but I can't help it. And look!" She pointed to one of her costumes. "There's a rip along the zipper. More bad luck!"

"Not bad luck, just bad stitching," said Barbie with a grin. "Do you have a needle and thread? I can fix this in no time at all."

Allie found her sewing kit and gave it to Barbie. Sure enough, in just a few minutes, Allie's skating outfit looked perfect.

"Thanks, Barbie," said Allie.

"Allie," said Barbie gently, "I want you to think about something. Do you remember how upset you were when you didn't win a trophy at last year's championships?"

"Do I ever!" Allie said. "I knew that I was good enough to win, but I made stupid mistakes because I wasn't thinking."

"And what happened at the next competition?" Barbie asked.

Allie smiled. "I won first place. Thanks to you, and to my skates!"

"No. You won first place because you trained hard. You had a strong body and a strong, determined mind. What's missing now is this one pair of skates. You don't need them. But you *do* need to believe in yourself. Don't lose everything you've worked so hard for over a pair of skates."

"I'll try my best, Barbie. I promise," said Allie. "But I don't know if I can."

"Well, *I* know you can," said Barbie, smiling.

After she left the room, Barbie thought about what had happened. She wanted Allie to stop relying on the skates. But she really wanted to solve the mystery.

"I'll talk to the Australian coach tomorrow," Barbie said to herself. "But right now, even coaches need some sleep!"

Chapter Five

The next morning, the skaters went for one last practice at the Palais de Neige. The exhibition round of the SuperSkate competition would take place that afternoon, and the team was excited.

All that was missing was a pair of lucky skates.

But Barbie was relieved to see Allie skating well in her backup skates. As for Julia, she was skating incredibly well. Her jumps were tighter and cleaner than ever before. She landed three triple toe loops perfectly, one after the other.

At one of the breaks, Julia skated up to

Barbie. "Do you think I could put a few triple toe loops in my program?" she asked, out of breath.

"Definitely," said Barbie. "That's the kind of difficult move that will win you higher scores. You really looked wonderful out there. What changed?"

Julia grinned and smoothed her pink skirt. She looked embarrassed. "I overheard your pep talk to Allie last night. And I really thought about what you said. I think if we just believe in ourselves, we all can win. And right now, I feel lucky enough to win first place!" She zoomed onto the ice, waving.

Suddenly Barbie heard a shout. Allie was sitting on the ice, rubbing her ankle. Her face was twisted in pain.

"What happened?" Barbie asked as she helped Allie off the ice.

"It's my ankle!" Allie said, taking off her purple mittens to unlace her skates.

"I'll take her to the trainer," Christie offered. "Allie should get off her foot. Then we should

get ice on her ankle right away."

"Thanks, Christie," said Barbie. "Hang in there, Allie! You'll be okay."

But Barbie wasn't so sure. "This might be serious," she thought. "I'd better tell Meg to be ready to take Allie's place. Tracking down those missing skates will have to wait."

Barbie found Meg in the locker room. Meg was reaching inside the last locker in the top row. Barbie noticed that it was the same locker that had been stuck the day before. Meg jumped when Barbie called her name.

"Boy, you're tense today!" Barbie teased.

Meg took a deep breath. "Look, Barbie, I've been meaning to tell you something," she began. But Barbie stopped her.

"Give me a minute first," said Barbie. "We might have a serious situation here." Then she told Meg about Allie's ankle.

Meg's hand flew to her mouth. "Oh, no!"

she cried. "You mean Allie might not get to compete? But she's number one in the world! She's worked so hard."

"I know," Barbie said. "It's not fair. But at least we're lucky we have you to step in."

Meg sat down on a bench. She looked up at her coach. "Barbie, do you think Allie hurt herself because she's still so upset about her skates?" she asked.

"Allie's trying to get her mind off them," said Barbie. "But that can be pretty hard. I think the missing skates are hurting her **concentration.** That may be why she's been falling."

Suddenly the door flew open, and Christie burst in. "Great news! The trainer said that Allie only strained some muscles. She should be fine for tomorrow."

Meg breathed a sigh of relief.

"Thank goodness!" said Barbie. "Now all we have to do is make sure her confidence is in good shape, too, without those skates."

"Still no sign of them?" asked Christie.

"No," replied Barbie. "And at this point, she has to realize she can do her very best with or without that pair of skates."

Barbie turned to Meg. "Well, I guess it was a false alarm. Thanks for being ready. But what were you going to tell me?"

"Um, nothing," replied Meg. "Nothing important. I'm going to find Allie and try to cheer her up." She ran out of the locker room and Christie followed.

Barbie sat down to think. "Why was Meg so nervous earlier at that locker? Why was Julia suddenly skating so well? How did Pam's sticker get into the jammed locker?" Maybe it was time to pick up the trail of the missing skates again.

Barbie found one of the Australian skating coaches inside the ring. Quickly Barbie explained about the missing skates.

"No, I didn't notice anything unusual in the locker room," the Australian coach told her, "except that one skater, the one with the blond hair, seemed to be nervous about something. I thought it was probably just the pressure of the competition."

"Oh, you must mean Meg," Barbie explained. "But Meg's an alternate," Barbie thought. "She knows she's probably not going to compete. Why would she be nervous?"

"Anyway," the Australian coach continued, "when my assistant took our team's skates out of one of the lockers, she *did* notice something strange."

"What was that?" asked Barbie.

"She found an extra pair of skates in the locker," the coach replied. "We took them along with our skates to be sharpened. I figured one of our girls would claim them."

Barbie thought for a moment. "Do you mind if I take a look at those skates?" she asked the Australian coach.

"No problem," answered the coach as they headed toward the locker room. Barbie had a feeling the mystery was about to be solved.

The coach showed Barbie the extra pair of skates. Then Barbie turned over the tongue of one skate.

"Uh-huh. Just as I thought," Barbie whispered. There was a heart inside the tongue. Then she turned over the other. In the same place on the tongue was a chrysanthemum sticker.

Barbie knew what she would find underneath the sticker, but she peeled it back anyway. And she was right. Another heart, identical to the first.

These were Allie's lucky skates!

The other coach was puzzled. "But why would anyone put a sticker on the tongue?" she asked. "And how did your skates get mixed in with ours?"

"I'll tell you all about it sometime, but not now," Barbie said as she shook the other coach's hand. "Thanks for your help. Tell your team that

I expect they'll really give us a run for our money. Good luck!"

Barbie hurried to Allie and Julia's room. She was hoping her whole team would be in the dorm. There would be just enough time to settle this mystery before the exhibition round.

Chapter Six

When Barbie got back, she quickly gathered the team in Allie and Julia's room.

"Before the exhibition round, I want to tell you how proud I am of all of you," began Barbie. "Every one of you has been giving a hundred percent. You've come a great distance on your own. Now I want to make sure we can go the distance as a team."

Then Barbie handed Allie her skates. "That's why we need to talk about these."

"My skates?" Allie turned over one of the tongues. "They are! There's a heart! But wait a minute! What's this sticker doing in the other one?"

"Hiding the heart," explained Barbie.

"I don't get it," said Allie. "And why would anyone try to hide only one of the hearts?"

"Well, the other sticker fell off," said Meg.

Barbie looked at her. "Meg can explain the whole thing." She put her hand on the young skater's shoulder. "Go ahead. It's all right."

Meg took a deep breath. She ran her fingers through her hair. "I really didn't mean to take them," she began. "It just happened. After I broke my ponytail holder during practice, I went to get a new one in the locker room. I noticed Allie's gold gym bag, and I got to thinking about how we borrow each other's shoes."

"Go on," said Barbie. Allie was staring right at Meg.

"So I told myself it would be the same thing to borrow her skates to see if they could be lucky for me," Meg continued. "I wanted to see if they

43

could help me skate like she does. So I put my back-up skates in a locker and took her lucky skates."

"But the skates didn't help, did they?" said Christie softly. "In fact, that's when you kept falling."

"Right," agreed Meg. "They fit fine, but I felt all wrong in them. I took them off and came in to put them back. But Christie had already taken our skates to the sharpener's. Then I heard voices."

"Is that when you put on the stickers?" Barbie asked.

Meg nodded. "The stickers Pam gave me when we were shopping were still in the pocket of my jacket. It was on the bench, right next to me."

"But why did you want to hide the hearts?" asked Allie.

"Because everyone knows about your lucky skates," replied Meg. "Someone could have stolen them for real. I wanted to protect them until I could come back for them later. So I took my backup skates out of the locker. Then I put Allie's lucky skates in the locker and pushed them way back. I closed the door partway but didn't slam it so it wouldn't lock."

"Then what happened?" asked Christie.

"I left as the Australian coaches were coming in," explained Meg.

Barbie continued. "Meg didn't know that the Australian skaters were storing their skates in the same locker. Allie's skates were picked up with theirs and brought to the sharpener's," explained Barbie. "And that's why Meg was so surprised when she found the locker empty. That was the clue that told me you were holding something back, Meg. That, and the sticker."

Meg looked away. "I really didn't mean to hurt you, Allie. When I thought you weren't going to be able to skate, I was so upset. It would have been all my fault."

"When I told you Allie might not be able to skate, you didn't act happy for yourself," said

Barbie. "You were really upset. I thought something might be going on with you and the skates. But your attitude told me you would never hurt her or anyone on purpose."

"Still, I'm sorry, Allie," Meg said.

Allie touched Meg's arm. "It's okay, Meg. I understand. Actually, I'm the one who's sorry," Allie said. "I've been so wrapped up in finding my lucky skates that I've been forgetting my skate mates! Now that the skates are back, I feel that I don't even need them. I actually like my backup skates better because the others are getting worn out. Besides, I don't need those hearts to know my parents love me. I know that in my *own* heart. Nothing can take that away."

"There's one more thing that puzzles me," Barbie added. "How did Allie's backup skates get in her gym bag?"

Julia spoke up. "I think I can answer that. I put both pairs of Allie's skates in the bag. It didn't occur to me to mention it before. It didn't seem important. All I was thinking about was wanting some of Allie's luck. I didn't take your skates, Allie, but I sure thought about it."

"It's all right, Julia," Allie told her.

The four young athletes were quiet. Meg brushed away a tear.

Then Pam said, "Well, I didn't take your skates either, Allie. Want to know why?"

"Why?" everyone asked.

"Because they would be *miles* too big for me!" joked Pam.

Everyone laughed, and the tension was broken.

"Now let's get over to the Palais de Neige and skate our hearts out!" cried Barbie.

Chapter Seven

Outside the Palais de Neige, all of the teams
lined up for their entrance. Barbie was at the front of
the American group, behind the flag carrier. As she
marched with her team, she couldn't help thinking
how relieved she was to have the missing-skates
mystery finally solved.

When all the teams had entered the colorful
skating rink, the crowd stood up and cheered. Soon
the competition began.

During the next few days, the American team
skated as they never had before.

Allie sailed across the ice with her arms

stretched wide and her head tilted to the sky. She landed each of her jumps perfectly. Before long, everyone knew the words *Allie-Oop*.

With her bouncing curls and bright smile, Juli was also a favorite. Each movement she made had spunk and style all its own. And Pam was known as the little skater with the big spirit. She dipped and whirled across the ice in her shiny blue costume. Barbie was so proud of her team. She knew they had learned a lot on their first trip to Paris.

It wasn't long before the team was in the staging area. It was sometimes called the "Kiss and Cry" area because athletes and their coaches sat there when they heard their final scores.

The group was anxiously waiting for Allie's long program scores. She had been the last competitor and had been in perfect form.

"Allie Moreno!" the announcer's voice boomed. "Five point nine, five point nine . . ."

Meg grabbed Pam's arm. "Where are the

sixes?" she hissed. "She deserves sixes!"

"Shh! I can't hear!" said Pam.

"Six point oh," the announcer continued. Then he repeated "six point oh" over and over and over. When he was through, Allie had been given the highest score out of everyone for the long program!

"ALLIE-OOP!" the crowd shouted.

The applause and whistling made Barbie's ears ring. She hugged Allie tight. "First place!" she said. "And without any lucky skates!"

Tears in her eyes, Allie cried, "I'll never need lucky skates again, thanks to you."

Christie hugged Allie and then grabbed Julia's hands. "And you won second place, Julia! They're going to start calling you the 'Comeback Kid.'"

"Come back from where?" laughed Barbie. "She never stopped being a champ! And that goes for the rest of you. Pam, you would have had third place if not for the Australian skater."

Then Barbie put an arm around Meg. "Even

though you didn't compete, you helped us pull together as a team," Barbie told her. "And next year—watch out, everyone! Here comes Meg!"

"You made us a team, Coach," said Meg.

"No, you did it together," Barbie said firmly. "You're all champions, and you're world-class wherever you go!"